Sol the Slug's

NIGHT BEFORE
CHRISTMAS

Written By
Lucy Banks
Illustrated By
Aless Baylis

Sol the Slug's Night Before Christmas is the winner of Amazon's UK competition to find a modern day version of the festive classic *Twas the Night Before Christmas.*

"I think there is a lot to be learnt from creatures like slugs; they are universally disliked but offer something rather lovely to the world. It is a story about acceptance and inclusivity, to look at the world differently and realise that regardless of appearance, or in this case sliminess, everybody is remarkable."

Lucy Banks, Author

'Twas the night before Christmas
The tree sparkled bright.
The presents sat gleaming
In warm candlelight.

But out in the kitchen,
The floorboards were cold
And deep underneath,
Were crawling with mould.

Sol didn't mind it -
He loved the grime.
For he was a slug,
With the slimiest slime.

At midnight exactly
Sol squeezed through the grooves,
And up into the dark
Kitchen he oozed.

He sashayed a trail
To the bright Christmas tree.
"It's pretty," he thought,
"But it's not for me."

Sol sludged to the table,
Saw the sweets piled up high.
"They look very tasty,
But not for this guy."

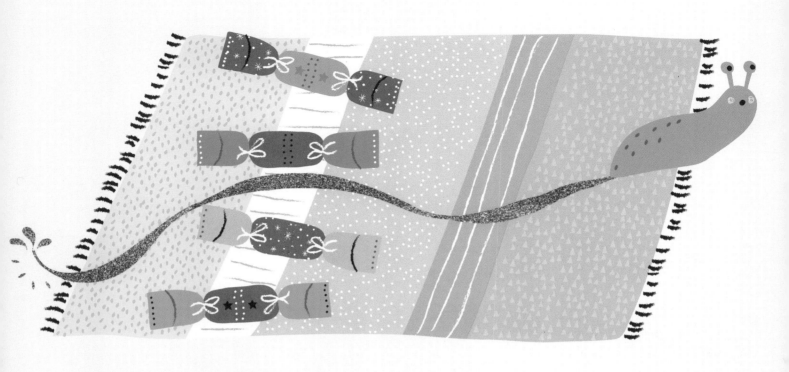

He slipped past the crackers
Arranged on the rug
"Wondrous!" he thought,
"But not for a slug."

"All this festivity,
Is not for our sort.
If we joined the fun,
We'd only get caught!"

"They'd salt us or boil us,
And shout and say no!
Then turf us outside
In the cold winter snow."

It's sad, he thought,
As he started to slither,
Leaving a trail
Like a bright moonlit river.

Leaving a trail like a bright moonlit river

Sol slid to the fireplace
Surrounded by holly.
"How lovely," he thought,
"So spiky and jolly!"

"But all this good fun,
Is not for our kind.
Ah well," Sol sighed,
"We must try not to mind!"

As he turned away,
A noise made him stop.
A rolling rumble
Came from up top.

A big, booming voice
Then after, a face;
And a big-bellied man
Landed in the fireplace!

Sol shrank away
In panic and fright.
"Don't let him spot me
On this festive night!"

But to his surprise,
The jolly voice said,
"Well, hello there, Sol,
Why aren't you in bed?"

The man's eyes twinkled
Like two festive lights.
He crouched beside Sol,
"Don't fear, I don't bite!"

Well, hello
there, Sol,
Why aren't you
in bed?

"It's the night before Christmas
I'm here to bring joy!
What would you like
From Santa, my boy?"

Sol's antennae trembled,
He was all of a quiver,
When he tried to speak
It came out as a shiver.

"I'm only a slug,"
He finally mused.
"Christmas isn't for us,
I'm feeling confused!"

Santa sat down,
Shaking his head.
"You're wrong, little Sol,"
He finally said.

"Christmas is for you,
And me," Santa smiled.
"And for every man,
Woman and child."

13

"It's for giraffes and wombats,
Crocodiles and cats,
Bears, mice and birds,
And big, flapping bats."

"It's definitely Christmas
For you, little slug.
Why, you are quite
My favourite bug!"

"I am?" whispered Sol,
Mouth wide with surprise.
"How can that be?
You're telling lies!"

"You," chuckled Santa
"Are an artist extraordinaire.
Look at the masterpiece
You've left over there!"

Sol turned to his trail
Which led out the door,
Glittering like tinsel
All over the floor.

"Angel-tracks," Santa said.
"Aren't you clever!
Why, they make the room
More lovely than ever."

Sol smiled then,
Beaming with pride
For he was an artist
At this Christmastide!

He glided to bed.
Beneath the kitchen floor.
Rolled into a ball
And started to snore.

Next morning, he woke
To thunderous feet.
As children ran in to
Get something to eat.

Then Sol saw it,
Laid down in the dim.
A piece of bright paper
Addressed just to him!

"Dear Sol", it read,
"Your talents are great,
The children will love them,
When they are awake.
You're hidden, forgotten,
But remember this.
Your talent lives on
With each surface you kiss.
Every trail that you leave,
Every path you unwind,
Is a magical treat
For others to find.
Wherever you roam to,
How near or how far.
Don't ever forget
How special you are.
When you next think
Christmas is not for you,
Read this letter,
And remember what's true."

From that day on, Sol
Made sure each Christmas day,
Was decorated
With trails bright and gay.

Painted tracks that
Spelled good cheer,
At this, the happiest
Time of the year.

And the people soon realised,
There's beauty to find,
In even small creatures
All covered in slime.

THE
END!

Lucy Banks is a professional copywriter and has been writing creatively since she was 19. Originally from Bishop's Stortford, Lucy now lives in Exeter, Devon with her husband and two young sons.

Printed in Poland
by Amazon Fulfillment
Poland Sp. z o.o., Wrocław